D1154907

CAN YOU FIND THE JERSEY DEVIL?

AN INTERACTIVE MONSTER HUNT

BY BLAKE HOENA

CAPSTONE PRESS
a capstone imprint

Published by Capstone Press, an imprint of Capstone.
1710 Roe Crest Drive, North Mankato, Minnesota 56003
capstonepub.com

Library of Congress Cataloging-in-Publication Data is available
on the Library of Congress website
ISBN: 9781666336887 (hardcover)
ISBN: 9781666336894 (paperback)
ISBN: 9781666336900 (ebook PDF)

Summary: Wild rumors are circulating in southern New Jersey. Stories are swirling
about weird hoofprints appearing in the Pine Barrens, a mysterious winged creature
flying around Leeds Point, and something sinister haunting Barnegat Bay. Could
these tales of terror mean the legendary Jersey Devil is on the prowl? It's up to YOU
to find out! With dozens of choices, you can follow the clues to the end. Which
path will YOU CHOOSE to discover the truth?

Editorial Credits
Editor: Christopher Harbo; Designer: Sarah Bennett;
Media Researcher: Svetlana Zhurkin; Production Specialist: Katy LaVigne

Image Credits
Alamy: Matthew Corrigan, 6; Dreamstime: Julie Feinstein, 66, Mdeebs1336, 84;
Getty Images: Enrique Aguirre Aves, 69, Hulton Archive, 74, Joe McDonald,
59, Peter Johansky, 40, Spiritartist, 100; Library of Congress: 102; Shutterstock:
Africa Studio, 90, Big Creative Studio, 106 (bottom), Christos Georghiou, 107
(top), Daniel Eskridge, cover, back cover, 1, Danita Delimont, 99, Debby Wong,
105, Erin Cadigan, 88, Fotofilia Maciej Pazera, 44, Grigoriy Pil, 34, jakkapan, 112
(back), Joe McDonald, 28, Karel Bock, 93, LMcCabe, 78, Long1k, 62, maxpro,
31, mipop, 106 (top), muratart, 53, 90 (inset), Ola-ola, 107 (bottom), Peggy
Hazelwood, 19, Peter Hermes Furian, 10, PTZ Pictures, 12, Rainer Fuhrmann,
49, Sketched Images, 107 (middle)

Printed and bound in the USA.   4882

TABLE OF CONTENTS

ABOUT YOUR ADVENTURE

YOU are a cryptozoologist who studies legendary creatures from around the world. When you see reports online that a strange creature known as the Jersey Devil has been spotted in New Jersey, you decide to head out to the Garden State to hunt it down. Will you be able to find proof that this weird, winged beast really exists?

Chapter One sets the scene. Then you choose which path to read. Follow the directions at the bottom of the page as you read the stories. The decisions you make will change your outcome. After you finish one path, go back and read the others for new perspectives and more adventures.

Turn the page to begin your adventure.

Depictions of the Jersey Devil vary, but the creature is often described as having a goatlike head, batlike wings, hoofed feet, and a long, forked tail.

CHAPTER 1

MONSTER HUNTER

You're a monster hunter, or—as some people say—a cryptozoologist. You've stomped through forests hunting for Bigfoot. You've roamed the Scottish Highlands in search of the Loch Ness Monster. You've chased after all sorts of mythical beasts from krakens to chupacabras. While you haven't found proof that any of these monsters exist—at least not yet—one day you hope to.

That is your goal. Your ultimate dream!

That is why you are sitting down at your computer once again doing research. Today, your focus is on New Jersey's legendary Jersey Devil. Scrolling through reported sightings has piqued your interest in this mysterious cryptid from the Garden State.

Turn the page.

The Jersey Devil has been lurking around New Jersey since the 1700s. Unfortunately, nothing you've read so far provides definitive proof that the monster actually exists.

Most of the stories are from people who say they saw a large creature that kind of looked like a winged kangaroo. Some people took blurry photos of a dark, shadowy figure flying overhead. Others posted low-quality, fuzzy video footage of a two-legged beast.

As a seasoned monster hunter, you know that a secondhand story, a bad photo, or an out-of-focus video is often the only proof you'll ever get. But you believe that with your skills and experience as a cryptozoologist, you can uncover proof that the Jersey Devil is more than a mythical beast. So you are determined to hunt down this creepy cryptid, no matter what it takes.

To start, you message fellow cryptozoologists in the New Jersey area. You want to know the best locations to search for the creature, and there's no better resource than the locals. The people you contact have also been searching for the Jersey Devil, and some even claim to have seen the creature.

First you hear back from Gabe. He's a fearless monster hunter who once joined you on a search for the Hodag—another creature of myth.

Gabe tells you of the Pine Barrens, where most of the Jersey Devil sightings have occurred. This vast wilderness area covers much of the southern part of the state and is a perfect spot for a mythical beast to hide.

Then Magdala messages you about Leeds Point, the birthplace of the Jersey Devil legend. She's a blogger and researcher who knows everything about strange cryptids.

Turn the page.

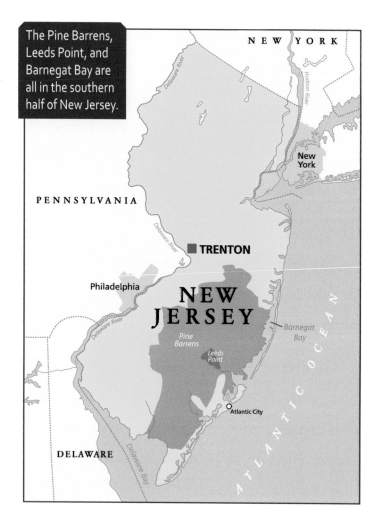

The Pine Barrens, Leeds Point, and Barnegat Bay are all in the southern half of New Jersey.

Leeds Point is on the eastern side of the state, near the Atlantic coast. It's where the Leeds family once lived, and legends say the beast is one of their descendants.

Lastly, you receive a text from Jeremy. He's new to the monster-hunting biz, but he has posted some great stuff about the mysterious Wampus cat—so you know he's legit.

Jeremy tells you stories about Jersey Devil sightings at Barnegat Bay, along the state's eastern coast. They are some of the most outlandish tales you've heard yet. Someone actually claimed to have seen the Jersey Devil walking along the beach with a ghostly pirate.

All three places feel like promising leads to begin your investigation. The people you contacted gave good reasons to visit each one of them. But who will you meet up with as you search for the fabled Jersey Devil?

To meet Gabe in the Pine Barrens, turn to page 13.
To meet Magdala at Leeds Point, turn to page 41.
To meet Jeremy at Barnegat Bay, turn to page 67.

The vast forest of New Jersey's Pine Barrens is believed to be the home of the legendary Jersey Devil.

CHAPTER 2

THE PINE BARRENS

From your research, you've learned that the legend of the Jersey Devil goes back hundreds of years. But it wasn't until the early 1900s that the cryptid truly became part of pop culture. Early in 1909, newspaper reports told of mysterious, hooflike footprints found in the snow around southern New Jersey. Some hoofprints were even discovered up on the rooftops of buildings.

These reports set off a craze of sightings. All over southern New Jersey and in Pennsylvania, Delaware, and Maryland, people claimed to have seen a creature with bat wings. Some descriptions said it stood on two legs and looked somewhat like a kangaroo. Others said the beast looked similar to a deer.

Turn the page.

In addition to the sightings, there were also reports of dead pets and chickens. All of the animals were believed to have been killed by the monster people were calling the Jersey Devil.

Back then, folks armed with rifles searched throughout the Pine Barrens for signs of the creature. Unlike them, you decide to head there with cameras to hunt down the Jersey Devil.

You meet up with Gabe in Pemberton Township, in the southeastern part of the state. The Pinelands National Reserve is not far from town. You're surprised that such a vast wilderness area is so near New York City and Philadelphia. The area is covered in pine forests and wetlands, and filled with an amazing variety of wildlife.

"It's also a great place to camp," Gabe tells you. "There are even hiking and biking trails running throughout the Pine Barrens."

Before setting off, you need to plan how to go about your search. You could camp in the Pine Barrens. That would allow you to set up your motion-sensing cameras in hopes of getting some footage of the Jersey Devil. Or you could rent a mountain bike. Then you'd be able to cover more ground in your search for the creature.

To set up camp, turn to page 16.
To rent a mountain bike, turn to page 29.

You've spent many nights out in the woods. You're not afraid of camping, and Gabe has everything you need for a couple of nights.

You add your motion-sensing cameras to his pile of gear. Your surveillance equipment will capture some great footage of whatever might be lurking in the Pine Barrens.

Then you set out, and you quickly realize why the area is also known as the Pinelands. It's covered in thick pine forests with stretches of swampland. By the time you reach your campsite, the sun is dipping toward the horizon.

"We'd better hurry," Gabe says, "if you want to get your cameras in place before dark."

You quickly pitch your tent. Then, as you pull out your surveillance equipment, you hear a distant cry.

Scccrrreee-aaahhh-aaahhh!

The screech sends shivers down your spine.

"What was that?" you ask Gabe. "It's not like any animal I've ever heard."

"That's because it's not an animal," Gabe replies. "That's the Jersey Devil. I've heard its call before."

Scccrrreee-aaahhh-aaahhh!

This time, the creature sounds closer, like it's just on the other side of a clump of trees.

The sun is about to set. You still have time to set up your cameras. Maybe whatever is out there will wander near enough for you to get some video. Then again, maybe following the cries into the darkening woods will be your best chance to get proof that the Jersey Devil truly exists.

To keep setting up your cameras, turn to page 18.
To go investigate the sound, turn to page 21.

You stop what you are doing and look in the direction of the calls. There is a dark forest between you and whatever is out there.

You know better than to go running across unfamiliar terrain in the dark. You won't be able to see simple hazards, like tree roots that could trip you or marshes that you could sink into. Not to mention the potentially dangerous monster that might be out there somewhere.

"Do you want to check it out?" Gabe asks.

You shake your head no.

"No point in stumbling around in the dark," you say. "Let's get the cameras set up. They have a night-vision mode and will be able to pick up whatever is out there."

You place your motion-sensing cameras in the woods around your campsite. Then you hunker down in your tent.

In a matter of minutes, you link your laptop to the cameras. Then you sit back and watch them throughout the night. But to your disappointment, you don't see anything noteworthy. Just a family of raccoons scurrying through the forest.

The next morning, before the sun has risen, you head over to where the cries came from the night before. In the dim light you find a spot where some pine needles had been disturbed. In the bare earth you see hooflike prints.

These could've been made by the Jersey Devil, you think.

Many animals have cloven hooves that are split in two.

Turn the page.

Glancing around, you don't see any more tracks. The ground is covered in pine needles. You could spend hours, or even days, in the Pine Barrens and not find more evidence. But you've heard strange screams and now see hoofprints! What more proof do you need?

You could tell the story of what you heard and post photos of the hoofprints. Even though you aren't sure about what made the sounds or prints—or if they are connected—you hope they are proof enough that the Jersey Devil exists.

Then again, what if nobody believes you? Perhaps it would be better to keep looking. It might take a lot of time—time you could spend looking for other monsters. But you may also find more convincing evidence than what you've already discovered.

To post your pictures online, turn to page 23.

To keep looking, turn to page 25.

"Forget about the cameras," you say, turning to Gabe. "Let's see what's making that noise!"

You grab your smartphone and rush into the night. Gabe follows.

Your heart is pounding. Usually you spend hours staring at a video screen, waiting for something exciting to happen. But the cryptid you're hunting might be just through a thicket of trees.

Scccrrreee-aaahhh-aaahhh!

You run faster as the cries get nearer and louder.

You're racing over unfamiliar ground and—in your excitement—aren't as careful as you normally would be. It's also getting dark. You can't see very well. You step wrong on something hidden by shadow—a tree root? You feel your ankle twist, and pain shoots up your leg.

Turn the page.

"Ahhhggg!" you cry out as you crash to the ground.

Gabe is quickly at your side. He pulls you to your feet, but you can't put any weight on your injured leg. Gabe helps you back to camp. By the time you get there, your ankle is swollen to the size of a softball.

"Looks bad," Gabe says.

You have Gabe take you to the nearest hospital. A doctor quickly confirms that you didn't break anything, but you suffered a serious sprain. The injury will keep you off your feet for weeks. You won't be able to stomp around the woods looking for the Jersey Devil, so your search has ended, for now.

THE END

To read another adventure, turn to page 11.
To learn more about the Jersey Devil, turn to page 101.

The Jersey Devil is just one of many cryptids on your list to track down. The more time you spend in these woods, the less time you have to hunt down other creatures. The cries you heard last night and the hoofprints are also more evidence than you typically find on one of your outings. So you are excited to share your story.

You take photos of the hoofprints. Then you show them to Gabe.

"It's gotta be the Jersey Devil," he says. "Remember those old newspaper stories?"

Yeah, you think. They mentioned hoofprints like these being seen in the snow. You feel even more confident that you've found proof the monster exists. You don't even wait to head home. That night, at Gabe's place, you type up your story and upload the photos you took.

Turn the page.

But not long after posting your story online, you start to receive negative feedback.

It's probably just a deer, one commenter says about the hoofprints.

Another asks, *Are you sure it wasn't an owl making that noise?*

The comments make you realize that what you posted really isn't much better than the photos you've seen from other people. Honestly, you have no idea what made the noises you heard or the hoofprints. So you have to admit that your expedition was a failure. The evidence you found wasn't enough to convince anyone of the Jersey Devil's existence.

THE END

To read another adventure, turn to page 11.
To learn more about the Jersey Devil, turn to page 101.

"Hey, Gabe," you shout. "Look what I've found."

Your companion comes rushing over.

"It's gotta be the Jersey Devil," he says. "Remember all those old newspaper reports about people finding hoofprints in the snow?"

"Yeah," you say. "But I wonder which way it went. There aren't any more tracks."

"Maybe it's up in the trees," Gabe says.

Then you remember. The Jersey Devil has wings. It can fly!

You and Gabe begin stomping around the area, scanning the trees for any sign of the creature.

After about an hour, Gabe turns to you. He puts a finger to his lips. "Shhhh."

"What is it?" you whisper.

Turn the page.

He points to a tree about a hundred feet away. Up in its branches sits a large, shadowy figure. In the dim morning light, it's difficult to see clearly. You could sneak closer to where the creature is perched and try to get a picture. But if you make a sound, you might scare it away.

Another option is to use your smartphone to take video of whatever is up in the tree. It might be a little blurry from this distance, but at least you would have some proof to show the world.

To sneak closer to the creature, go to page 27.
To take video of the creature, turn to page 35.

You worry that any noise might scare off the creature and ruin your chance of learning what it is. But you need to get closer to get a good photo.

You tell Gabe to stay put. Then you slowly make your way toward the creature. You are careful not to make the slightest sound. Up ahead, you see some fallen brush that you can hide behind. From there, you might be close enough to get a picture of the creature in the tree.

You bend down and slink toward the cover of the brush. As you do, you hear a strange rattling. Then you feel a sharp sting on your wrist.

You look down and are surprised to see a brownish-colored snake. You're even more surprised to see the blood on your arm.

You forget about the creature in the tree and rush back to Gabe.

"I think I got bitten by a snake," you tell him.

Turn the page.

Timber rattlesnakes live all across the eastern United States. They can be found as far north as New York and as far south as northern Florida.

"What kind of snake?" Gabe says. "There are timber rattlers in these woods, but they're rare."

But that's what bit you! You're sure of it. And even though timber rattler bites are rarely deadly, you need to seek treatment.

Gabe rushes you to a hospital. The doctor tells you it will take time for you to recover from the venom in the snake's bite. For now, your monster hunting is put on pause.

THE END

To read another adventure, turn to page 11.
To learn more about the Jersey Devil, turn to page 101.

While camping with Gabe would allow you to set up your motion-sensing cameras, you have no idea where the Jersey Devil might be. It's been seen throughout the Pine Barrens. It could be anywhere in this vast wilderness, which spreads across much of south-central New Jersey.

So you believe renting a mountain bike and heading out on your own will allow you to cover more ground and give you a better chance of spotting the creature. To prepare, you get a map of the area's trails and a day's worth of supplies.

Before you leave, Gabe points out a few spots on the map. They are places people have seen the Jersey Devil. You plan to check out as many of them as you can.

"I'll be back by nightfall," you tell Gabe. Then you hop on your bike and you're off.

Turn the page.

Throughout the day, you take breaks to eat and take photos of the area. You definitely want to document your expedition.

But after riding around for most of the day, you haven't had any luck in your search. You could keep exploring the Pine Barrens. Although it is getting late, there are still a few spots on the map where you haven't stopped.

You also wonder if the rattling of your mountain bike over the rough trails could be scaring away anything that might be out in the woods. You could find a spot to hunker down and wait. Maybe if the woods are quiet, the Jersey Devil will come out of hiding.

To keep riding around, go to page 31.

To stop, turn to page 33.

Riding a mountain bike is sometimes the best way to cover a lot of ground while exploring a large, wooded area.

You decide to keep exploring on your mountain bike. You know that finding a monster from folklore isn't a simple task. Otherwise there would already be proof that this creature exists. It takes patience and persistence, but mostly time. Lots and lots of time.

You continue to ride around the woods. You are so focused on your search that you fail to realize how late it is getting. As the sun sinks below the horizon, darkness quickly spreads across the Pinelands.

Turn the page.

That's when you finally decide to head back. But in the darkness, it's hard to read the map or clearly see the trails. At some point, you puncture a tire on a rocky outcrop. Even worse, you discover you forgot to pack a tire repair kit.

You're stuck, and you have no way to get back. You know that wandering around in the dark will only get you more lost, especially at night.

At least I have food and water, you think as you try to reassure yourself that you're not in any immediate danger.

Throughout the night, you hear all sorts of strange noises and animals calling out. You don't know whether any of them could be the Jersey Devil. But for now, your search is over as you are more worried about surviving the night.

THE END

To read another adventure, turn to page 11.
To learn more about the Jersey Devil, turn to page 101.

Since you haven't seen anything riding around, you decide to try a different approach. You head to one of the spots where the Jersey Devil has reportedly been seen. You park your bike and then hunker down in the forest.

You sit on a fallen tree trunk in a small clearing and wait. And wait. And wait . . .

This is a big part of what you do as a cryptozoologist. You wait. Most often, your waiting comes to nothing. But this time, after about an hour, you're in luck. You hear a distant screech.

Ssscccrrreee-aaahhh!

You feel goose bumps on your arms. It's unlike any animal you've heard before. Slowly, you start creeping through the woods toward the sound. You are both afraid and excited about what you might find.

Turn the page.

Tricks of the light can make it difficult to photograph and identify wildlife in a dense forest.

Sssccccrrreee-aaahhh!

Up in a tree you spot a large, shadowy figure.

You're too far away to see it clearly, and it's also getting dark. But you could try using your smartphone to zoom in and capture video of it before it flies off.

Or you could head back to your bike. That way if it takes flight, you'd be able to give chase.

To take video, go to page 35.

To chase the creature, turn to page 36.

You know that any sound could scare off the creature—so you pull out your smartphone and start taking video of what you see. After a few moments, the creature spreads its wings. They are huge—many feet wide. Then you watch as the gray, shadowy figure flies off.

That was incredible, you think after its gone.

Wasting no time, you head home and upload the footage to your blog. Your fellow cryptozoologists are excited to see it. Many think it's proof that the Jersey Devil exists. Others think it might be an owl or other large bird.

While your video isn't definitive proof that the monster exists, you achieved one goal. You've created a buzz with some amazing footage of what just may be the elusive Jersey Devil.

THE END

To read another adventure, turn to page 11.
To learn more about the Jersey Devil, turn to page 101.

You are worried that whatever is up in the tree might fly off. So you hurry back to your bike. As soon as you reach it, you hop on and slowly head in the direction of the creature. You try to get some photos, but the pine forest is just too thick for you to get a clear shot.

Then the creature spreads its huge wings, screeches—*Scccrrrreeeahhhh*—and takes flight!

You shift gears and race off after it.

The creature's wingspan is huge—maybe six feet wide. You can see its shadowy shape soaring just above the treetops.

At first, the creature glides along the path. But soon it veers toward a dry creek bed. If you stop, it will get away. But if you chase it, you will be riding over very rough terrain.

To stop, go to page 37.
To keep chasing the creature, turn to page 38.

You hit the brakes and skid to a stop on the edge of the trail. Then you watch the creature disappear as it flies off.

You are frustrated that the creature, whatever it was, got away. But you don't want to go off the trail. Dry creek beds can be thick with rocks and fallen trees, and you don't want to risk an accident.

You head back to meet up with Gabe that night. He's excited to hear about your adventure.

"Sounds like you saw the Jersey Devil," he says. "A bummer you didn't get proof, though."

Sadly, you know Gabe's right. While your adventure makes a good story, it's not proof that the Jersey Devil exists. Then again, sometimes a good story is better than nothing at all.

THE END

To read another adventure, turn to page 11.
To learn more about the Jersey Devil, turn to page 101.

You are so close to achieving your goal. The Jersey Devil, or at least what you think is the legendary creature, is just overhead. You don't want to stop chasing it now.

You turn off the path and into the dry creek bed. As you dart around large rocks, you feel your mountain bike bounce violently over the uneven ground.

You risk a glance up to see where the creature is. At that moment, your front tire hits a fallen log in the creek bed. The jolt sends you flying over the handlebars and into a nearby tree. On impact, everything goes black.

When you wake, you're lying in a hospital bed. A doctor is standing over you and examining a bandage on your head.

"Where am I?" you mutter.

"Take it easy," he says. "You suffered a pretty bad concussion."

Your heart falls into the pit of your stomach when you hear those words. You know that you'll need time to recover—and that your hunt for the Jersey Devil is over.

THE END

To read another adventure, turn to page 11.
To learn more about the Jersey Devil, turn to page 101.

Leeds Point, nestled along New Jersey's eastern coastline, is considered the birthplace of the legendary Jersey Devil.

CHAPTER 3
LEEDS POINT

As you suspected, Magdala turns out to be a great resource. She's done lots of research on almost every cryptid imaginable, and that includes the Jersey Devil. You message back and forth during the couple of days it takes you to plan your trip. She tells you all sorts of interesting facts about the cryptid you're about to hunt.

It's also called the Leeds Devil, she texts.

The most common rumors surrounding the creature say it was the thirteenth child of a witch nicknamed Mother Leeds. She lived in the area back in the 1700s. Before her child was born, stories say she cursed it, shouting, "Let this one be the devil!"

Turn the page.

Shortly after the child was born, it grew hooves and wings. Its head became horse-like, and it had a whip-like tail. Then it flew up the chimney and disappeared into the night. The creature has haunted the area ever since.

Leeds Point, of course, is named after the Leeds family. The area is part of Galloway Township, just north of Atlantic City.

U can visit the remains of the Leeds house, Magdala tells you. *Or I could introduce u to people who've seen the JD.*

It would be cool to see where the folk legend was born. The remains of the Leeds house might be a good place to start your investigation. Then again, people who claim to have seen the Jersey Devil might lead you right to the creature.

To visit the Jersey Devil's birthplace, go to page 43.
To talk to eyewitnesses, turn to page 50.

You're excited to see the place that gave birth to the Jersey Devil's legend. You can't think of a better way to start your hunt for the creature. So you agree to meet Magdala in Galloway, and she drives you over to the ruins.

"I haven't been there in years," she tells you on the way. "There might not be much left to see."

Magdala stops her car at the end of Moss Mill Road. You grab a video camera, and then the two of you stomp off toward the woods. You follow an old, overgrown path leading into the forest.

Turns out it's not too far of a walk to get to the ruins. And as Magdala said, there is not much to see when you get there.

The clearing is covered in scattered fallen trees—almost like someone, or something, knocked them over. In the middle of it all there's a sunken area where a house once stood.

Turn the page.

After years of neglect, moss and vegetation often hide any lingering clues left behind in an abandoned dwelling.

As you draw closer to the sunken area, you find some crumbled, moss-covered bricks. You're not sure, but it looks like they might have been part of a house's original foundation.

"Some stories say that the Jersey Devil killed Mother Leeds after it was born," Magdala says. "Yet other stories say it would return here from time to time to see her."

If this is a place that the Jersey Devil comes back to, it would be a good place to set up some of your motion-sensing cameras. You might get lucky and capture the creature on video.

But it takes a lot of time to set up your cameras, and you would also like to explore around the area. It's been hundreds of years, but maybe there are still some clues in and around these ruins that could help in your investigation.

To set up your cameras, turn to page 46.
To search the ruins, turn to page 48.

The Jersey Devil was born hundreds of years ago. There is really nothing left of the house it once lived in. And you're sure hundreds of people have searched this area for clues. There probably isn't much to find. But if rumors say the creature comes back here from time to time, then maybe it's worth setting up your cameras.

As you head back to Magdala's car to get your equipment, you cross paths with a woman who lives in the area.

"Have you seen any signs of the Jersey Devil around here?" you ask her.

"No, not for a long time," she says. "But did you hear about the most recent sighting?"

Both you and Magdala shake your heads.

The woman goes on to tell you a farmer claimed a monster with red, glowing eyes had tried getting at some of his chickens.

Sounds like a classic Jersey Devil sighting, you think.

The news of this recent sighting sounds almost too exciting to resist. You wonder if you should change your plans and go talk to the farmer.

On the other hand, the ruins are the birthplace of the Jersey Devil. Perhaps sticking with your plan to set up your cameras in a place the creature has been rumored to visit is the better bet.

To investigate the farmer's sighting, turn to page 51.
To continue setting up your cameras, turn to page 64.

It's not often that people know where stories of a cryptid began. The creature's origins are often a muddy mix of legends and hearsay. But this place represents the birth of the Jersey Devil legend. You have to investigate further.

You circle the dip in the ground where the house once stood. You kick at the area where you found the crumbling bricks. Then, as you brush away some leaves on a pile of logs, you feel a sharp pain on the back of your hand.

"Ow!" you shout, pulling it away.

Magdala rushes over. The two of you look at your hand and see two tiny puncture marks.

"I think I got stung," you say. "Twice!"

"Nah, that looks more like a spider bite," Magdala replies. "And we do have some venomous ones around here, like yellow sac and brown recluse spiders."

As you look at the wound further, you notice your hand is swelling up. The area where you got bitten is itchy.

That's when Magdala decides you should go to the hospital. Neither of the spiders she mentioned are typically deadly, but you can't risk having a serious reaction. For now you'll have to put your monster hunting on hold until you receive medical attention.

THE END

To read another adventure, turn to page 11.
To learn more about the Jersey Devil, turn to page 101.

As a cryptozoologist, you know it's important to talk to the people who claim to have seen a cryptid. So when you arrive at Galloway Township, Magdala takes you to a local café. There you meet a couple folks who are happy to talk about their encounters with the Jersey Devil.

One woman says a horned creature has been stalking the woods behind her house.

"I hear its screams almost every night," she says. "I'm sure it's that Leeds Devil."

Another person says a local farmer has seen a creature trying to get into his chicken coop.

"He told me it has red, glowing eyes," the person says.

Both sound like classic Jersey Devil sightings.

To check out the farmer's sighting, go to page 51.
To check out the woman's sighting, turn to page 54.

Along with having horns and batlike wings, reports of the Jersey Devil say it has red, glowing eyes. You can just imagine the creature swooping down into the farmer's chicken coop. That had to have been a scary sight, and since it happened recently, it would be a great sighting to investigate.

You tell Magdala of your plan to check out the farmer's sighting. Since it's getting late, she's unable to go with you, but you thank her for her help.

Then you head on over to the farm and introduce yourself to the farmer. You go on to tell him that you heard about the creature that he's seen around his farm. You also ask if it's okay for you to set up some motion-sensing cameras around his chicken coop.

"If I can get some video of it," you explain, "then maybe we'll have proof that the Jersey Devil is real."

Turn the page.

"Sounds good to me," the farmer says.

Then you get to work.

By the time you're finished, it's dark. You decide to find a hiding spot to wait and see if the creature appears. Sure, it's exciting to capture a possible cryptid on video. But it would be thrilling to see one in person.

You hunker down behind a wood pile and wait. Next to research, waiting is what you spend most of your time doing. So you wait. And wait. And wait . . .

Just as you feel yourself dozing off, a noise startles you. It sounds like the whooshing of wings. But it's coming from behind you.

You turn to look. Part of you is fearful that it's the Jersey Devil creeping up behind you. But you're also a little bit excited about the possibility.

Many animals have eyes that appear to glow in the dark when they reflect light.

Out of the corner of your eye, you see a pair of red, glowing dots in the night. They are up in a tree and staring in your direction.

You're unsure what to do. You could try pulling out your smartphone to get a picture. Any sudden movement might scare off the creature. Or you could just stay still and hope the creature flies into the view of your cameras.

To pull out your smartphone, turn to page 56.

To stay still, turn to page 58.

Among the many descriptions you've come across, the Jersey Devil is described as having horns. The woman's sighting sounds like an intriguing one to investigate.

Because it's getting late, Magdala can't join you, but she wishes you luck. Then you head over to the woman's house.

"The sounds usually come from over there," the woman says, pointing toward a clump of trees behind her house. As she heads inside, you get to work. You brought along some surveillance equipment, including motion-sensing cameras and recording equipment. You begin setting up along the edge of the woman's yard.

As you are working, a bloodcurdling shriek startles you.

Scccrrreee-haa-haa!

What was that? you wonder as you feel the hairs on the back of your neck stand up.

You could continue setting up your cameras in hopes that whatever is out there in the dark will eventually wander this way. But maybe it won't, and you will miss out on an opportunity to capture proof of the Jersey Devil's existence.

Or, you could head off into the woods looking for the source of the sound. You're not sure what's out there, or if you should be wary of any other dangers. But you've been out looking for monsters in dark and creepy woods before, so you're not afraid.

To continue setting up, turn to page 60.
To hunt down the sound, turn to page 62.

Part of you wonders if you're more afraid of the creature than it is of you. It keeps staring at you with its red, unblinking eyes. Now that it sees you, you don't know if the creature will swoop down toward the chicken coop. You also don't know if it will swoop down and attack you.

What you do know is that this is your best chance to get a photo.

Slowly, you reach into your pocket to pull out your smartphone. Ever so slowly, you lift the phone up to take a picture.

You snap a few shots before the creature screams.

Scccrrreee-haa-haa!

Then you see it lift its shadowy wings.

It's about to attack! you think and instinctively cover your head with your arms.

There is a sudden whooshing of large wings as the creature lifts into the sky and flies off.

You swing your phone around to take some more photos, but it's too late. The creature is gone.

In the end, none of the pictures you took turn out great. They are blurry and shaky and too dark to make out any details. But the ones of the red eyes up in the tree spark a lot of interest from other cryptozoologists when you post them online. Many think it was the Jersey Devil. Others say there must be another explanation— an owl, maybe. But no matter what anyone else believes, you were successful in adding to the creature's legend. Even more people think it's real after seeing your photos.

THE END

To read another adventure, turn to page 11.
To learn more about the Jersey Devil, turn to page 101.

You stay as still as you can, even though a mix of fear and excitement makes it difficult. No matter what, you don't want to miss out on a sighting, even if it might be a dangerous monster.

And your patience pays off—kind of. As you sit as still and quiet as you can, the creature opens up its wings. In the shadows of the tree, they appear huge. Then the creature screeches, *scccrrreee-aaahhh*, and launches itself into the air.

In the blink of an eye, the beast swoops down at you. For a fearful moment you think it's about to attack and that you need to run for your life.

But then the creature whooshes overhead. That's when you see it clearly. It's a large owl.

While you are bummed about not actually seeing the Jersey Devil, a part of you is also relieved. At least you didn't have to come face to face with a deadly monster.

You pull out your phone to report back to Magdala that you only saw an owl.

That's too bad, she quickly replies. *But at least the farmer will know what's been after his chickens.*

You're not too disappointed. Part of being a monster hunter is also disproving false leads, like this one. Maybe you'll have better luck next time.

THE END

To read another adventure, turn to page 11.
To learn more about the Jersey Devil, turn to page 101.

Every time you hear a strange noise in the night it reminds you of all the horror movies you've watched. Most cryptozoologists love them! But in far too many, people bumble through the dark and head straight toward danger.

You do not want to be a victim like in your favorite horror movie. So you do not go running off into a dark forest where a strange creature is calling out.

Instead, you finish setting up your cameras. Then you hide out in the woman's garage and link the cameras to your laptop. On your computer screen you can see whatever the cameras pick up.

Throughout the night, you see something shadowy moving about in the trees. It's too far away for you to get a clear image of it, but you definitely see horns—or maybe they're antlers. You aren't sure.

The next morning, you thank the woman, pack up your gear, and then head home. Once you're back behind your desk, you review the footage further.

You can see a figure moving through the night. You even see flashes of what you think might be horns. But none of it is enough proof for you to be certain it's the Jersey Devil. So you say exactly that when you post the video online. Instead of telling people you have evidence of the monster's existence, you let the world decide.

THE END

To read another adventure, turn to page 11.
To learn more about the Jersey Devil, turn to page 101.

You know a great opportunity when you see one. Or in this case, hear one. It's not often you're this close to what might be the monster you're looking for. So you do not want to miss the chance to see it and maybe even get some photos.

You rush off into the night. You follow the strange sounds farther and farther into the dark forest.

Scrrreee-haa-haa!

A forest at night can be filled with hidden and unexpected hazards.

You're trekking through unfamiliar woods, with no idea where you are heading. The farther you go the more lost you become, until you hear a shriek right behind you.

Scrrreee-haa-haa!

* * *

What happens to you, nobody knows. There haven't been any reported human victims of the Jersey Devil, but rumors swirl saying you may be the first. As the stories go, you were investigating what a woman thought was the Jersey Devil. Your camera gear was found partially set up. There were even footprints leading into the forest. But after weeks of searching, your body has yet to be discovered and you become part of the monster's legend.

THE END

To read another adventure, turn to page 11.
To learn more about the Jersey Devil, turn to page 101.

Since you had already settled on setting up your motion-sensing cameras, you stick to that plan. After all, this is the birthplace of the Jersey Devil. What better place to stake out?

While you get your cameras positioned around the ruins in the clearing, Magdala goes back to town to get snacks for the night. Then you link the cameras up to your laptop. You can see what the cameras see on its monitor.

By the time you're done, it's getting dark. You head back along the overgrown path. You find Magdala waiting for you next to her car at the end of Moss Mill Road. Then the two of you get in the car and wait. And wait. And wait . . .

Throughout the night, you take turns watching the computer screen. Every so often, some critter will set off one of the cameras. But you do not see any sign of the creature you are looking for.

Determined to keep trying, you and Magdala decide to stick it out a few more nights. But the results are the same the next night, and the night after that.

After four nights of staking out the birthplace of the Jersey Devil, you admit defeat. There are other monsters to hunt down, and you are having no luck finding evidence that the Jersey Devil is real. So you decide to call it quits and head home. Maybe on the next monster hunt, you'll chase after the most recent lead and have better luck.

THE END

To read another adventure, turn to page 11.
To learn more about the Jersey Devil, turn to page 101.

Barnegat Bay extends about 42 miles (68 kilometers) down the eastern coast of southern New Jersey.

CHAPTER 4

BARNEGAT BAY

Of the stories you've heard about the Jersey Devil, the one Jeremy tells you seems to be the most far-fetched. But that's the reason it intrigues you. If you find evidence of a ghost *and* the Jersey Devil, you will double the respect you get from other cryptozoologists.

The coolest part, Jeremy texts, *is that some stories say the ghost is headless.*

No way! you reply.

Jeremy goes on to explain that people believe the infamous pirate Captain Kidd buried his treasure somewhere along shore of Barnegat Bay. This waterway is on the eastern coast of the state. As legend has it, he left behind one of his crew to guard the treasure.

Turn the page.

But some stories say Kidd beheaded the pirate so his ghost would guard the treasure, Jeremy adds.

That's just crazy, you reply.

I know! Right? Jeremy texts back.

But in your years of hunting monsters, that is not the strangest story you've heard. Hearing wild tales is just part of being a cryptozoologist.

Jeremy goes on to say that supposedly the pirate ghost and the Jersey Devil became friends, and they walk the beach together. If that's true, you want to see it for yourself. So you agree to meet in New Jersey's Stafford Township, not far from the coast.

You pack your gear and head out. Soon, you are traveling along a road that cuts through the Pine Barrens, a vast wilderness of bogs and pine forests. And it's one of the places the Jersey Devil commonly haunts.

Then, as sunset nears, something strange happens. You see a large, shadowy figure fly out from the forest. It swoops low over your car. You swear you hear its claws scrape against the roof.

You skid to a stop and jump out. You have your smartphone ready to take video of whatever it might be. But all you can see is a shadowy figure flying off into the distance.

It's gotta be the Jersey Devil, you think.

Turn the page.

As daytime turns to twilight, it can be difficult to clearly identify large, winged creatures that pass overhead.

You are stunned. The very creature you're after just flew overhead. You could chase after it. It's not often you see the creature you're after this close up, so this could be your best chance to get proof it exists. But if you do, you will miss your meetup with Jeremy.

Still, chasing after some strange creature into the middle of unfamiliar wilderness could be risky. You have no idea what dangers may be lurking out in the forest. If you keep your planned meeting with Jeremy, you will at least be with someone who knows the area, so you won't get lost. He also knows the hidden dangers you need to be wary of.

To chase after the creature, go to page 71.
To continue on to meet Jeremy, turn to page 73.

Jeremy is a cryptozoologist like you, and you're sure he will understand if you can't make it tonight. After all, you are here to hunt down proof of the Jersey Devil's existence. And if it truly just flew overhead, you have to go after it.

You send Jeremy a quick text saying you'll meet him tomorrow. Without waiting for a reply you grab a camera and flashlight from the car. Then you are off, plunging into the darkness of an unfamiliar wilderness.

This isn't the first time you've done something like this. It's just part of being a cryptozoologist. But you have to be careful whenever you are stomping through a dark, unfamiliar landscape. There may be dozens of hidden dangers, and it could be very easy to get lost.

As you get farther into the woods, it gets harder to see the creature. But every so often it gives off a loud screech that you can follow.

Turn the page.

Scccrrraaawww! Scccrrraaawww!

Every time you hear it, you feel a shiver run down your spine.

As you continue on, the landscape changes. The forest continues to your right, but you can make out a clearing to your left. It's hard to see in the dark, so you are unsure which is the best way to go. The forest has trees that the creature might eventually land in, but it might be easier to hike through the clearing.

To go into the forest, turn to page 75.
To go through the clearing, turn to page 78.

As you watch the creature fly away, you make a hard decision. While it would be exciting to go stomping through the forest after it, you would feel bad about ditching Jeremy.

Also, as an experienced monster hunter, you know the dangers of heading off into strange terrain. It's best to explore unfamiliar places with a guide, and for you that would be Jeremy.

So you get back in the car and continue on. But once you see Jeremy, all you can talk about is what happened on the road.

"A lot of people have had similar experiences," he says. "There have been thousands of reported sightings of the Jersey Devil in the Pine Barrens."

Jeremy goes on to say that it is dangerous to be wandering around in the Pinelands at night. It's easy to get lost and there are swampy areas that are pretty tough to hike through.

Turn the page.

Hearing Jeremy's opinion makes you feel better about not pursuing the creature you saw. Sometimes it is just better to play it safe.

The two of you talk a little more. Then you agree to meet up again tomorrow, just before sunset, near where Oyster Creek flows into Barnegat Bay.

"It's one of the places people think Captain Kidd might have buried his treasure," Jeremy explains.

Turn to page 83.

According to legend, Captain Kidd buried his treasure before he was captured, convicted, and executed for piracy. But to this day, no one has ever found it.

You head toward the trees. Not only are the Pine Barrens known for their pine forests, but the area is also covered in wetlands. You figure you'd be less likely to walk into a swamp and get wet if you stay in the forest. Plus, the creature you're following is bound to land sometime and will likely perch in the trees.

Scccrrraaawww! Scccrrraaawww!

You keep following the sound of its cries until you see a large, black shape perched in a tree. Just as you had hoped, the beast has come home to roost! Unfortunately, the night is too dark and the creature is too far away for you to clearly see what it is. But you can think of nothing else that could be as big. It has to be the Jersey Devil.

Suddenly, the creature turns its head toward you. You see two, red glowing eyes glaring right back at you.

Turn the page.

A shiver runs down your spine. You begin to wonder if you truly made a mistake. You're stomping through the woods chasing after a dangerous monster, and now you are face to face with it.

But you've been in situations like this before. Fear only stops you for a moment. You pull out your camera and zoom in as best you can. You take photo after photo of the dark creature in the tree.

Then, as you shift your feet to get a better view—*CRACK*—you step on a twig.

The sound spooks the creature, and it flies off, farther into the Pine Barrens.

It's dark out, and you're in an unfamiliar wilderness. Plus, you just took some photos that you're excited to review. So you head back to your car.

Once you get back, you are exhausted. That was more work than you expected, but you also got what you think are some great pictures. While a little dark and obscured by the dense forest, they still clearly show a large, winged creature. Maybe they are enough to prove that the Jersey Devil exists.

You could cancel your plans to meet up with Jeremy and return home to post your photos. They are more proof than you get on your typical expeditions, and there are many other monsters you'd like to hunt down.

Or you could still meet up with Jeremy. He lives in the area, is more familiar with the Jersey Devil, and might have some thoughts on the photos you took.

To post your photos online, turn to page 80.
To meet up with Jeremy, turn to page 82.

Hiking through a dark, unfamiliar landscape is difficult enough. So instead of heading into the woods, you walk toward the clearing. Not only will it be easier to walk through, but you'll be able to see better. Some light from the moon shines down on you, so you might even have a better chance of seeing the creature.

You've only hiked a short distance into the clearing when you take a step and hear a loud splash. Suddenly, the ground seems to disappear under you.

SPLOOSH!

Boggy wetlands are often dotted by puddles and potholes. Their depth can be deceiving.

Not only are the Pine Barrens known for thickets of pine trees, but there are areas of boggy wetlands. That is what you just found, and you crash into the water.

Luckily, the water is not too deep. But as you flail around, you lose your smartphone and your flashlight. On top of that, the rest of your gear is wet and much of it is ruined.

Worst of all, in all the confusion you have lost track of which direction you came from. You're unsure how to get back to your car. As your body begins to shiver uncontrollably, you realize it is going to be a long, miserable night of stomping around the woods in cold, wet clothes. Even if you make it out alive, you know your hunt for the Jersey Devil is over.

THE END

To read another adventure, turn to page 11.
To learn more about the Jersey Devil, turn to page 101.

Oftentimes, you don't even get any photos of the would-be creature you are searching for. And most photos that people have posted are much less convincing than the ones you took. So you are excited to head home and take a better look at them.

You send Jeremy a message saying that you won't be meeting up with him at all. You explain that you've already spotted the Jersey Devil, and he can check out the evidence on your website.

That's cool, he texts back.

Then you head home and upload your photos.

But shortly after posting them, you are surprised to receive some negative feedback. To make matters worse, it's Jeremy who is posting comments! He is discrediting you. He says that the photos are probably just an owl. He also says they look digitally altered.

You're shocked. You don't know if he's angry that you didn't meet up, or if he's upset that you spotted the Jersey Devil without him. Either way, you feel like you've been punched in the gut.

You know there is a lot of competition among cryptozoologists. Everyone is trying to be the first to prove a cryptid exists. Everyone is trying to take the best photos and capture the best footage. But Jeremy's comments are so upsetting that you end up taking your photos off your website.

THE END

To read another adventure, turn to page 11.
To learn more about the Jersey Devil, turn to page 101.

Once you get back to your car, you text Jeremy. You tell him about the ordeal of stomping through the Pine Barrens.

You're lucky you didn't get lost, he says.

Then you tell him about the photos.

Send them to me, he says.

Jeremy thinks they are great photos. But he can't tell whether the shadowy figure is actually the Jersey Devil or just an owl. He says it's probably a good thing you didn't post the pictures until you've found more proof. Then he texts about meeting tomorrow, just before sunset, where Oyster Creek flows into Barnegat Bay.

Sure thing, you reply. *Why there, specifically?*

Some people think Captain Kidd's treasure is buried there, he says.

As you wait to meet up with Jeremy, you spend time on some research. That's a key part of what you do as a cryptozoologist. You need to find everything you can about the monsters you're hunting and the area you'll be exploring. Sometimes, you even uncover stories you hadn't heard about before.

For such a small state, New Jersey has numerous stories of legendary creatures. None are quite as well known as the Jersey Devil. But there's the headless pirate that Jeremy mentioned.

You also read about the Black Dog and the Golden-Haired Girl. Both are ghosts that haunt the New Jersey coast.

The Black Dog drowned off the coast of Barnegat Bay. It has been spotted roaming the beaches of the Jersey shore.

Turn the page.

The Golden-Haired Girl has been seen staring out across the Atlantic Ocean. Some believe she is looking for a long-lost love.

People have reported seeing the Jersey Devil with both of these ghosts. Maybe after you find proof that the Jersey Devil exists, you can search for one of them.

Before you know it, it's time to head out. You meet up with Jeremy in Waretown. It's a small town along New Jersey's coast. Oyster Creek runs through it and out into Barnegat Bay.

Oyster Creek stretches about 10 miles (16 km) inland from Barnegat Bay.

You and Jeremy hike to the mouth of the river. The area is mostly wetlands with a few housing developments off in the distance. There isn't a lot of cover and no good spots to put up motion-sensing cameras. They are what you usually use to stake out an area. With them, you can stay out of sight while monitoring what they pick up.

Instead, you and Jeremy find a spot to hunker down where you have a good view of the beach. Then you wait. And wait. And wait . . .

For some reason, scary cryptids like the Jersey Devil are almost always spotted at night. And as night spreads across the landscape, you hear the whoosh of wings above. Something large and gray flies overhead. Then it dips down toward the horizon, and you lose sight of it.

"What do you think that was?" you ask Jeremy.

Turn the page.

"I'm not sure," he says. "But it flew away from the beach, not toward it. And the beach is where people have seen the ghost pirate and the Jersey Devil together."

Jeremy seems pretty hung up on rumors of the Jersey Devil and the pirate. It is the story that brought you to this place, so maybe you should stick with it and keep an eye on the beach.

But you are really curious about the creature that flew overhead. Neither of you got a good look at it in the dark. It seemed huge, and maybe it was even the very monster you are looking for.

To stay on the beach, go to page 87.
To see what the creature was, turn to page 92.

Jeremy is pretty set on watching the beach for signs of the Jersey Devil.

"I've talked to a lot of folks who claim to have seen it here," he says.

He is the local expert, so you stick to your original plan. In the end, his hunch pays off.

As the light fades, fog rolls in. Only moonlight lights up your view of the sandy beach. Then out of the mist steps a shadowy figure. No! It's two shadowy figures.

"Look," Jeremy says. "The one on the right—the shorter one—doesn't have a head!"

You squint your eyes to get a better view, but it's dark and you're too far away to clearly see. You can't tell if what he claims is true or not. It could be a monster and a ghost pirate out there in the dark, or just two people strolling along the beach.

Turn the page.

A thick fog can often make people and objects appear to be something they are not.

You want to rush over to take photos of the creatures, but Jeremy holds you back.

"They will disappear if you make any noise," he warns.

So you take out your camara and try to zoom in on some shots from where you are. But whether it's the darkness or the fog rolling in from the ocean, the creatures in the photos are hardly noticeable.

"I have to get a closer look," you whisper to Jeremy.

"Okay, okay," he says. "But don't make a sound."

That's not an easy thing to do while you're stumbling about in the dark. Something brushes against your pant leg. The wet ground squishes underfoot. Every noise seems amplified by the stillness of the night. Then the figures suddenly disappear in a wisp of fog.

Jeremy rushes up to you.

"Did you see the one—the taller one—fly off?" he says excitedly.

You shake your head. In the dark and misty air, you couldn't see anything clearly.

"I'm going to post about this as soon as I get back to my computer," Jeremy says.

Turn the page.

You're not as sure as he is. In the photos you took, you can kind of see the figures in the background. But they aren't clear enough to definitively prove that you saw the Jersey Devil.

So while Jeremy posts that you two saw the Jersey Devil and the ghost pirate, you post a different story. You tell people that you saw "something," but that you aren't exactly sure what it was. You also include the pictures you took.

Most people who read your post are skeptical. They respectfully share their opinions of your photos, and many doubt that you actually saw the Jersey Devil.

People are less friendly to Jeremy. Many doubt his story. Some leave negative feedback. A few people call into question his skills as a cryptozoologist.

Your hunt for the Jersey Devil may have been a failure. But in the end, you're proud not to have made any false claims about the cryptid. People continue to respect your work as a monster hunter.

THE END

To read another adventure, turn to page 11.
To learn more about the Jersey Devil, turn to page 101.

"We can always stake out the beach another night," you tell Jeremy. "I want to see what it was that flew overhead."

"Fine, go," Jeremy says.

You can tell by the tone of his voice that he's not happy about your decision. But you can't let a possible lead go uninvestigated. Especially when it flew right over you! So you head in the direction that the creature flew.

While Jeremy doesn't stop you, he also doesn't join you. He continues to watch the beach. That means you are on your own.

Your progress is slow. A swampy area sits between you and whatever you saw. But the soft ground underfoot allows you to advance quietly.

Up ahead, you think you see a shadowy shape standing tall in the grass and shrubs. You crouch down and keep creeping forward.

Spotting and positively identifying an animal or creature camouflaged in a wetland environment can be challenging.

Then *SPLOOSH!* You step in a puddle. The water isn't very deep, only up to your ankles.

You peek above the grass and see that the shadowy figure is still there. It must not have heard you.

But in the darkness, you're a little unsure how best to move forward. You're ankle deep in water and fearful of making any noise that might scare the creature—or whatever it is—away.

Turn the page.

You're already wet, so you could just continue through the puddle and head straight for the creature. Or you could try skirting around the puddle and hope that you can find a drier path through the wetland. Whatever you decide, you don't want to take too long because you're worried that the creature could fly off at any moment.

To go through the puddle, go to page 95.
To go around the puddle, turn to page 97.

You don't want to waste time trying to find a drier path, so you keep moving forward.

Getting wet never hurt anyone, you think as you take another step forward.

SPLOOSH! The sandy muck sucks at your feet. Then another step. *SPLOOSH!*

The next step ends in a *SPLASH!* The mucky surface slips away under your feet. Water splashes all around. You are soaked and gasping for breath as you grasp for anything to help pull yourself out of the muck.

Suddenly, a hand wraps around your wrist. It's Jeremy. He pulls you out of the mucky mess.

"What happened?" he asks. But before you can answer, he says angrily, "I thought I saw two figures on the beach. But as soon as you started thrashing around out here, one of them flew away and the other disappeared into the fog."

Turn the page.

That's when you recall the creature you were searching for. You glance around, but there's nothing to be seen except for the distant glow of the housing developments.

Jeremy turns away and stomps off. When you get back to his car, he takes you back to Waretown, where you met up.

"Thanks for the ride," you say as you get out of his car.

"Bye," is all he says before driving off.

You stand there stunned. You stick around Waretown for a few hours and try to call Jeremy. But he doesn't return your calls or texts asking to meet up again. Without his help, you have to end your hunt for the Jersey Devil.

THE END

To read another adventure, turn to page 11.
To learn more about the Jersey Devil, turn to page 101.

You decide to skirt around the puddle, hoping to find drier ground. But that is not an easy task in a swampy area. Every time you set your foot down, you are not sure how far it is going to sink into the sandy muck.

But slowly, you get closer to the creature. Peeking through the grass, you can tell that the beast stands on two legs and is about four feet tall. It has a long, narrow head and a longer neck. Then it spreads its wings. It has a massive, six-foot wingspan! Surely this must be the legendary creature you seek.

Without warning, the beast leaps into the air! As it takes flight, you pull out your smartphone to take photos. Even while you are taking them you know you're still too far away, and it's too dark for the photos to turn out well.

Turn the page.

You rush back to show Jeremy the photos. He tries to hide his disappointment at not being with you.

"This is just what I need for my post about the Jersey Devil," you tell him.

"Yeah, cool," he says quietly.

The next day, you return home. You wish your photos were clearer, but you still post them online. You hope that someone might verify that the creature you found was the Jersey Devil. Within minutes, someone responds. They quickly point out that the creature in your images looks more like a crane, maybe even a sandhill crane.

After doing a little research, you come to the same conclusion. The narrow head, long neck, and massive wingspan are all telltale features of a sandhill crane. You found a bird—not a beast from the beyond!

Sandhill cranes have massive 6.5-foot (2-m) wingspans.

While that wasn't what you were after, you aren't upset. Being a cryptid hunter gets you out in the wilderness where you can appreciate all kinds of rare wildlife. This time you just were more of an ornithologist than a cryptozoologist!

THE END

To read another adventure, turn to page 11.
To learn more about the Jersey Devil, turn to page 101.

The Jersey Devil is sometimes referred to as the Leeds Devil because it was believed to be the child of a woman nicknamed Mother Leeds.

CHAPTER 5

HISTORY OF THE JERSEY DEVIL

Most stories trace the Jersey Devil's origins back to the Leeds family. Daniel Leeds moved from Great Britain to the New Jersey Colony in the late 1600s. Back then, little was known about what might be lurking in the unexplored wilderness of North America. As a result, people were often superstitious of anything they did not understand. They readily believed rumors that monsters and witches were real.

The most common story is that the Jersey Devil was the child of a woman nicknamed Mother Leeds. She was the wife of Daniel Leeds' eldest son, and many tales say she was a witch.

In 1735, while on the verge of giving birth to her thirteenth child, legend says that Mother Leeds shouted, "Let this one be the devil!" After the child was born, it grew horns, hooves, a whiplike tail, and wings. Some stories say it killed Mother Leeds and injured many people in the house. Then it flew up through the chimney and disappeared into the surrounding forest.

A more likely story involves Benjamin Franklin. In the early 1700s, both he and Titan Leeds, one of Daniel's sons, published popular almanacs.

Benjamin Franklin published his popular *Poor Richard's Almanack* from 1732 to 1758. It sold up to 10,000 copies per year.

In his book, Franklin taunted Titan. He claimed his rival had died and that Titan was just a ghost. Franklin's stories may have fueled the Leeds Devil legend. Since people already thought a strange, winged creature haunted the Pine Barrens, Franklin's tales led them to believe the creature was connected to the Leeds family.

Throughout the 1800s, there were only a few reported sightings of the Leeds Devil. Sometimes it was described as monkey-like and other times more like a dragon. But the creature was always said to have wings.

In 1909, newspapers in Philadelphia started new rumors about the beast. They reported strange, hooflike prints in the snow around Leeds Point. The articles also included drawings of a reptilian-like creature with wings standing on two legs. Around this time, the creature was increasingly being referred to as the Jersey Devil.

Then came Charles Bradenburgh, who owned the Ninth and Arch Street Dime Museum in Philadelphia. At some point, he had a stuffed kangaroo painted with stripes and fashioned with wings.

Bradenburgh put the fake creature on display in his museum as the Jersey Devil. Although it was eventually discovered to be a hoax, it further fueled stories of the creature. Soon, armed parties of hunters roamed the Pine Barrens looking for the beast.

Over the years, there have been many more reported sightings of the Jersey Devil. People claim to have seen a strange, winged creature flying overhead. They have reported hearing bloodcurdling cries in the Pine Barrens. While none of the reports have provided definitive proof of the creature's existence, they have kept the local legend of the Jersey Devil alive.

The New Jersey Devils' logo sports the iconic horns and forked tail of the legendary creature for which the team is named.

These days, the Jersey Devil has evolved from a frightening monster into more of an iconic figure for the Garden State. Its pro hockey team—the New Jersey Devils—is even named after the mythical monster. The cryptid has also inspired several horror movies and has appeared in TV shows and books.

We may never have proof that the Jersey Devil exists. But people's vivid imaginations and superstitions continue to keep this creature of folklore alive.

More Pine Barrens Creatures and Ghosts

Along with the Jersey Devil, the Pine Barrens are home to many legendary creatures and ghosts. Many of them, like M'sing, were born from American Indian stories. Others stem from people's superstitions about supernatural monsters and beasts that might be lurking in the tangled wilderness of the Pinelands.

M'sing

Lenape people living in southern New Jersey honored this forest god. It was said to be a deer-like creature with leathery wings. Some believe the Jersey Devil could be based on this fabled creature because they both have antlers or horns and wings.

White Stag of Shamong

Unlike other monsters roaming the Pine Barrens, this white deer is believed to be a good omen. One story says it saved some people aboard a stagecoach from plunging into a river on a stormy night.

The Black Dog

Legends say a cabin boy and his companion, a black dog, drowned off Barnegat Bay when the ship they were aboard sank. Ever since, people have claimed a ghostly black dog romps around the area's beaches.

Headless Pirate

The beaches of Barnegat Bay are one of the places the famed pirate Captain Kidd is believed to have buried his hoard of treasure. Legend says that he left behind one of his crew to guard the treasure. But the cruel captain beheaded the man, so now the ghost of a headless pirate haunts the area.

Atco Ghost

While driving through the Pine Barrens along Burnt Mill Road, superstitious folks believe you will see a ghost just outside the town of Atco. The ghost is a boy who was hit by a car. To make him appear, people need to honk their horns three times and flash their lights three times at a certain place on the road.

Golden-Haired Girl

She is a lonely ghost who haunts New Jersey's shores. She is seen staring out toward the ocean mourning a lost love. Some stories say she mourns the loss of her love while at sea. Others say she died in a storm. People claim they have also seen the Jersey Devil sitting with the Golden-Haired Girl.

Glossary

almanac (AWL-muh-nak)—a book published yearly that has facts on many subjects

amplified (AM-pluh-fyd)—made louder

bog (BOG)—a type of wetland that includes wet, spongy ground and pools of muddy water

concussion (kuhn-KUH-shuhn)—an injury to the brain caused by a hard blow to the head

cryptid (KRIP-tihd)—an animal or creature that people have claimed to see but has never been proven to exist

cryptozoologist (krip-tuh-zoh-AH-luh-jist)—a person who searches for evidence of unproven creatures such as the Jersey Devil

descendant (di-SEN-duhnt)—a person's child and a family member born after that child

elusive (ee-LOO-siv)—clever at hiding

expedition (ek-spuh-DIH-shuhn)—a journey made for a specific purpose, such as exploring a new region or looking for something

folklore (FOHK-lohr)—the traditional beliefs, legends, and customs of a group of people

hoax (HOHKS)—a trick to make people believe something that is not true

infamous (IN-fuh-muhs)—known for a negative act or occurrence

marsh (MARSH)—an area of wet, low land usually covered in grasses and low plants

mythical (MITH-i-kuhl)—imaginary or possibly not real

omen (OH-men)—a sign of something that will happen in the future

ornithologist (or-nuh-THOL-uh-jist)—a biologist who studies birds

proof (PROOF)—facts or evidence that something is true

skeptical (SKEP-tik-ahl)—unable or unwilling to believe things that other people believe in

superstitious (soo-pur-STI-shuhss)—believing an action can affect the outcome of a future event

surveillance (suhr-VAY-luhnss)—having to do with keeping very close watch on someone, someplace, or something

terrain (tuh-RAYN)—the surface of the land

venomous (VEN-uhm-us)—having or producing a poison called venom

wingspan (WING-span)—the distance between the tips of a pair of wings when fully open

Other Paths to Explore

>>> You are with Gabe while out camping in the Pine Barrens. He knows the area and has the necessary survival gear to spend a few nights in the wilderness. He also knows the local stories about the Jersey Devil. Imagine you do not have his help. How might this make your hunt for the monster more difficult? What would happen if you got injured and had no one to help you?

>>> All sorts of strange creatures and ghosts are rumored to roam the Pine Barrens. Imagine that while out in this vast wilderness area you spot something that is unlike any creature you've heard or read about before. Describe how the creature looks and sounds. Then explain how you would convince people of its existence.

>>> While doing research about the Jersey Devil, you come across the story about the Golden-Haired Girl. This is the ghostly spirit of a woman who is mourning her lost love that some people claim to have seen sitting with the Jersey Devil. How might you go about hunting for this pair? What sort of information would you try to dig up in your research? Whom might you ask to help you?

Read More

Borgert-Spaniol, Megan. *Cryptozoology: Could Unexplained Creatures Be Real?* Minneapolis: Abdo Publishing, 2019.

Finn, Peter. *Do Monsters Exist?* New York: Gareth Stevens Publishing, 2023.

Halls, Kelly Milner. *Cryptid Creatures: A Field Guide.* Seattle: Sasquatch Books, 2019.

Krensky, Stephen. *The Book of Mythical Beasts & Magical Creatures.* New York: DK Publishing, 2020.

Internet Sites

10 Things You Should Know About the Jersey Devil
theculturetrip.com/north-america/usa/new-jersey/
articles/10-things-you-should-know-about-the-jersey-devil

The Jersey Devil and Folklore
pinelandsalliance.org/learn-about-the-pinelands/
pinelands-history-and-culture/the-jersey-devil-and-
folklore

New Jersey Pinelands Commission—Jersey Devil
nj.gov/pinelands/infor/educational/facts/jerseydevil.shtml

About the Author

photo by Russell Griesmer

Blake A. Hoena grew up in central Wisconsin, where he wrote stories about robots conquering the moon and trolls lumbering around the woods behind his parents' house. He now lives in Minnesota and enjoys writing about fun things like history, space aliens, cryptids, and superheroes. Blake has written more than fifty chapter books and dozens of graphic novels for children.

Other Books in This Series